FIRST TIMES

Charles Ghigna
Lori Joy Smith

ORCA BOOK PUBLISHERS

Cataloguing in Publication information available from Library and Archives Canada

Issued in print and electronic formats.
ISBN 978-1-4598-1198-0 (hardcover).—ISBN 978-1-4598-1199-7 (pdf).—
ISBN 978-1-4598-1200-0 (epub)

First published in the United States, 2017
Library of Congress Control Number: 2017932489

Summary: A picture book that celebrates the important adventures children experience as they grow.

Orca Book Publishers is dedicated to preserving the environment and has printed this book on Forest Stewardship Council® certified paper.

Orca Book Publishers gratefully acknowledges the support for its publishing programs provided by the following agencies: the Government of Canada through the Canada Book Fund and the Canada Council for the Arts, and the Province of British Columbia through the BC Arts Council and the Book Publishing Tax Credit.

Cover and interior artwork created using watercolor, gouache and pencil.

Edited by Liz Kemp
Cover and interior artwork by Lori Joy Smith
Design by Jenn Playford

ORCA BOOK PUBLISHERS
www.orcabook.com

Printed and bound in China.

20 19 18 17 • 4 3 2 1

For Charlotte and Wes

—*Charles Ghigna*

To Sosi,
who made me a first-time mama.
It has been my life's joy to
share all of your first times.

—*Lori Joy Smith*

First times are
FUN times,
from summer to spring!

My first *slide* down the slide.

My first swing on the swing.

My first run with a kite
as it climbs to the sky.

My first *wish* on a star.

My first butterfly.

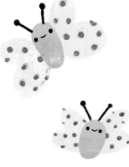

The first bubble I blow that floats on the air.

The first time I try to BRUSH my own hair.

The first time I
pick out
and **put on**
my clothes.

The first time I try to
BLOW
my own nose!

The first time I play a game that I choose.

The first time I finally tie my own shoes.

The first time I help my mother go shopping.

The first
time I
ride
my bike
without
stopping.

The first time I help my father make dinner.

The first race
that I run and I am the
WINNER!

The first time I *write* my name in the sand.

The first time I *catch* a ball in my hand.

The first time I **SWIM** across the big pool.

The first time I *walk*
with my friends to my school.

The first time
I **travel**
far, far away.

The first time
we hike and I
**lead the
way.**

The first time I SING a new song out loud.

The first time I dance
in front of a crowd.

The first time I get my very own pet.

The first time I bathe him—
and I get all WET!

The first time I pick a BOOK from the shelf.

The first time I read it all by myself.